TO SARA AND HANA CEPIĆ

AND LOVE TO MONIKA AND LUKA, MY TWO BIG BOUNCERS.

www.davidmelling.co.uk

WE LOVE YOU, HUGLESS DOUGLAS!

DAVID MELLING

A division of Hachette Children's Books

Hodder Children's Books

It was a bright and beautiful kind of day.

'A day for sharing with friends,' thought Douglas.

So he went out to look for someone to play with.

Only he couldn't find anyone.

Anywhere.

Until he heard a noise…

'Hello Flossie,' said Douglas. 'How did you get up there?'

Flossie took a deep breath.
'I was playing hide-and-seek with
**MY BEST FRIEND
LITTLE SHEEP** and I got
stuck and now he's lost and…'

'Don't worry,' said Douglas.
And he placed Flossie gently
on the ground.

Flossie gave Douglas a **THANK YOU HUG!**

'Please will you help me find Little Sheep?'
she sniffed.
'Of course I will,' said Douglas.

And together they headed off to do just that.

They soon passed the Old Barn and found Cow and her best friend preparing frothy-top milkshakes for everyone.

'Hellooo,' said Cow. 'Take a seat and we'll make you strawberry and banana smooOOOoo-thies!'

'We can't stop now, Cow,' said Douglas.
'We're looking for Little Sheep. Have you seen him?'

Cow looked under the table. 'Nooooo!' she said.
'Have you tried going down, through and round about?'

Douglas wasn't quite
sure what she meant but
thanked her all the same
and hurried on.

Douglas and Flossie made their way down the hill,
through the long, tickly grass towards Tall Tree Wood.

They were busy searching around and about when all of a sudden they were surprised by three flying bunnies!

'Good catch!' said Rabbit. 'Have you come to join our class, **BEST FRIEND BOUNCERS?**'

'No,' said Douglas. 'We're looking for Little Sheep.'

'Pity, I could do with a catcher for my big bouncers,'
Rabbit sighed. 'Well, if you're looking for sheep,
why don't you try Baa Baa Bush?'

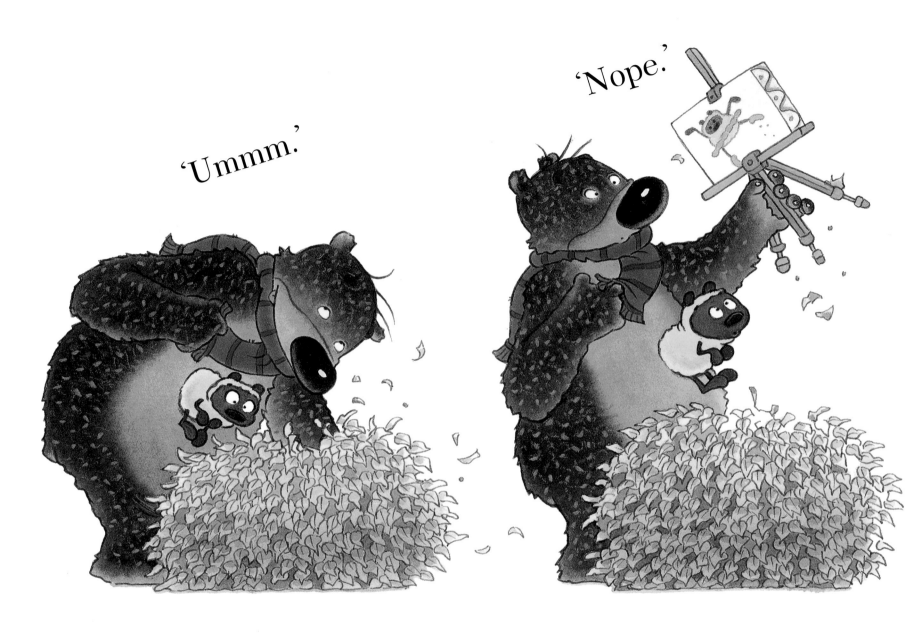

By the time they reached Baa Baa Bush, Flossie
was very excited.
'Let's see what we can find in here,' said Douglas
and he rummaged around in the leaves.

There was no sign of any sheep. But Flossie wriggled and squeaked and asked Douglas to look again…

'Found you, Little Sheep!'
cried Flossie.

'BEST FRIENDS TOGETHER AT LAST,'
smiled Douglas.

The two sheep looked so happy and trotted off
hand in hand.

Douglas waved them goodbye.
'I WISH *I* HAD A BEST FRIEND,'
he said.

Close by,
wise old Owl
heard his wish.

Douglas wondered why he felt so sad and sat down
to think for a while.

He was just about to head home when he heard
a rustling sound behind him…

Everyone was there!

'We heard you needed a best friend,' said Rabbit.
'So we all came to find you.'

Douglas realised how silly he had been.
'Of course, we're ALL best friends together.'

'WE LOVE YOU, HUGLESS DOUGLAS!'
everyone cried.
'And I love you too,' smiled Douglas.

I ♥ badges

We ♥ piggybacks

I ♥ muddy puddles

I ♥ drawing and painting

I ♥ ladybirds

I ♥ my mum

We ♥ bouncing

I ♥ my best friend

I ♥ pudding

I ♥ my dad

I ♥ books

We Love You, Hugless Douglas!
by David Melling

First published in 2013 by Hodder Children's Books

Text copyright © David Melling 2013
Illustration copyright © David Melling 2013

Hodder Children's Books
338 Euston Road
London NW1 3BH

Hodder Children's Books Australia
Level 17/207 Kent Street
Sydney NSW 2000

A catalogue record of this book is
available from the British Library.

ISBN: 978 1 444 90829 9 (HB)
10 9 8 7 6 5 4 3 2 1

Printed in China

Hodder Children's Books
is a division of Hachette
Children's Books.
An Hachette UK Company.

www.hachette.co.uk